THE EMPIRE STRIKES BACK®

A Storybook by
J.J. Gardner

Adapted from the Screenplay by
Leigh Brackett and Lawrence Kasdan

Story by George Lucas

SCHOLASTIC INC.

New York Toronto London Auckland Sydney

ISBN 0-590-06656-0

™ & ® & © 1997 by Lucasfilm Ltd. All rights reserved.
Published by Scholastic Inc.

12 11 10 9 8 7 6 5 4 3 2 1   7 8 9/9 0 1 2/0

Designed by Joan Ferrigno
Edited by Allan Kausch (Lucasfilm) and Ellen Stamper (Scholastic)

Printed in the U.S.A.   14

First Scholastic printing, February 1997

A LONG TIME AGO IN A
GALAXY FAR, FAR AWAY . . . .

It is a dark time for the Rebellion.
Although the Death Star has been destroyed,
Imperial troops have driven the Rebel forces
from their hidden base and pursued them across
the galaxy. . . .
Evading the dreaded Imperial starfleet, a group of
freedom fighters led by Luke Skywalker has established
a new secret base on the remote ice world of Hoth.
The evil Lord Vader, obsessed with finding young
Skywalker, has dispatched thousands of remote probes into the
far reaches of space. Unbeknownst to the Rebel forces, one of
the probes has headed for Hoth.

Commander Luke Skywalker galloped across the windswept ice slopes of Hoth on his tauntaun. He was tired and cold. He had been exploring the snowy slopes for half a day and still hadn't come across any life forms. That meant the chances were good that there were no Imperial troops on Hoth. The Rebel forces would be safe here.

He was about to return to the command center when he noticed a fiery object falling from the sky. Looking through his electrobinoculars, he watched the object crash behind a hill of snow. It was probably a meteorite.

"Echo Three to Echo Seven," Luke called into his comlink. "Han, old buddy, do you read me?"

"Loud and clear, kid," came the familiar voice of Han Solo. "What's up?"

"I don't pick up any life readings," Luke reported. "There's a meteorite that hit the ground near here. I want to check it out."

Luke clicked off his transmitter. Just then his snow tauntaun shuddered and let out a nervous whinny. Luke heard a monstrous howl all around him. A large shadow suddenly fell over him. Luke looked up. A huge three-meter-tall creature, completely covered with thick white fur, was now towering over him.

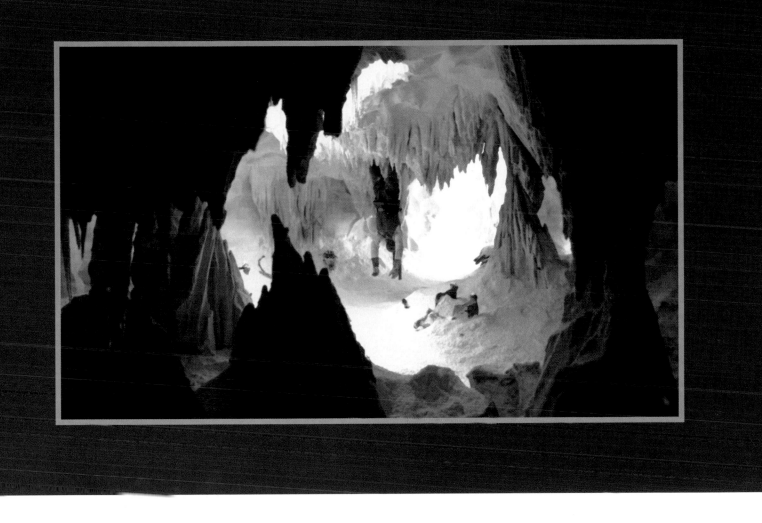

Before Luke could reach for his laser pistol, he was hit across the face by the creature's giant white paw. It was the last thing he felt before falling unconscious into the snow.

When Luke awoke he was dangling upside down. His feet were tied to the roof of an ice cave. His arms were extended just above the floor. He pulled himself up and tried to untie his feet, but could not. Exhausted, he let himself drop back into the hanging position.

Just then he heard the monstrous howl again. The same creature that had attacked him outside was now lumbering toward him from behind an ice pillar.

Luckily, Luke saw that his lightsaber was stuck a meter away from him. He tried to swing himself closer to the lightsaber, and strained desperately to reach it, but was unable to do so.

Then he squeezed his eyes shut tight and began to concentrate. Before long he felt the power of the Force flow through his body and reach his fingertips. He extended his fingers toward the lightsaber.

With the ice creature only centimeters away, the lightsaber jumped into Luke's hand. He ignited the weapon and cut himself loose from the ceiling. Landing on his feet, he swung the sword, wounding the ice creature. Then he ran out of the cave and into the dark evening.

But Luke was too weak to make it back to the Rebel base. He staggered away as far as he could, and then collapsed. He was barely conscious when he saw the ghostly figure of Ben Kenobi appear before him.

"Ben?" he asked weakly.

"You will go to the Dagobah system," said Ben.

"Dagobah system?" Luke muttered.

"There you will learn from Yoda, the Jedi Master who instructed me," said Ben. And with that Ben faded away just as mysteriously as he had appeared. Seconds later Luke blacked out.

When Luke regained consciousness he found himself inside a tank of gooey slime. He knew at once that he was in a bacta tank back at the command center. Someone must have found him in the snow and rescued him.

After he was sufficiently healed he was taken to a recovery room.

"Master Luke, sir!" C-3PO exclaimed upon entering the room. "It's so good to see you fully functional again!" Alongside the thin golden droid was R2-D2, C-3PO's companion. A happy series of beeps sounded from the little droid's dome-shaped head. "R2 expresses his relief, also," translated C-3PO.

Luke was already smiling when his friends Han Solo and Chewbacca entered.

"How are you feeling, kid?" asked Han. "You don't look so bad to me."

"Thanks to you," said Luke. He had learned that it was Han who had saved him.

Just then an alarm sounded in the station. "Headquarters personnel, report to command center," came a voice over the loudspeaker.

Han and the droids raced to the command center. There they joined Princess Leia and General Rieekan at a console screen.

"We've picked up something outside the base," explained the general.

"It's metal," said another officer.

"Then it couldn't be one of those creatures that attacked Luke," said Princess Leia.

"There's something very weak coming through," said the officer, as he listened to a strange beeping sound.

"This signal is not used by the Alliance," said C-3PO. "It could be an Imperial probe."

"It isn't friendly, whatever it is," said Han. "Come on, Chewie, let's check it out."

Han and Chewie followed the strange signal until they spotted a dark object floating across the snowy plains. Within seconds, the object caught Chewbacca in the sights of its laser weapon. But before it could get a shot off, Han fired a laser bolt, hitting the weapon from behind and shattering it.

"An Imperial probe," said Princess Leia upon hearing Han's description over the comlink.

"It's a good bet the Empire knows we're here," said Han.

After a brief conference, the Rebels decided to evacuate Hoth. It would be only a matter of time before the Imperial fleet arrived.

Light years away, Darth Vader entered the main control deck of his Imperial Star Destroyer. A signal had come through from the probe that his men had sent to the Hoth system. Vader hoped the signal meant that they had found the Rebel base. He hoped they had found Luke Skywalker.

"You found something?" Vader asked the officer in charge of the search.

"Yes, my lord," said the captain.

Vader looked at the image on the screen. "That's it," he said, pleased. "The Rebels are there."

"My lord," said the admiral. "It could be smugglers."

"That is the system," insisted Vader. "And I'm sure Skywalker is with them. Set your course for the Hoth system. Prepare your men."

Following orders, the admiral set the Star Destroyer to go to lightspeed.

On Hoth, the Rebel forces hurried to evacuate the ice world. It was decided that a small fleet of pilots would lag behind in their snowspeeders to make sure the rest of the Rebels got away safely.

But no sooner had the evacuation begun than a signal came over the computerscan in the control room. The Imperial fleet had just arrived out of hyperspace.

"Prepare for a ground assault!" General Rieekan ordered the Rebels.

Luke joined the other Rebel pilots as they climbed into their snowspeeders and readied to attack the invading Imperial soldiers. Just then a frantic voice came over Luke's comlink.

"Echo Station Three-T-Eight," came the voice. It was one of the Rebel officers stationed outside in the snow trenches. "We have spotted Imperial walkers!"

"Echo Station Five-Seven," replied Luke. "We're on the way." And with that, he and the other pilots blasted off in their speeders. In a short while they reached the snow trenches. Through his viewport, Luke could see that the Rebel ground team was being attacked by three huge robots. The robots, each as tall as a building, lumbered through the snowy slopes on powerful mechanical legs. They were blasting the Rebels with their laser cannons as they went.

Luke watched as one of the other Rebel snowspeeders raced directly ahead of him. It swooped between the legs of one of the walkers. The walker's head swiveled, catching the craft in its sights. Then it fired a laser blast at the snowspeeder, sending the speeder crashing in a ball of flames.

Luke knew that the walkers were going to be tough to beat. He swerved his ship toward one of them and blasted it straight on. But his laser bolts couldn't even dent the walker's armor.

"That armor's too strong for blasters," Luke called to the other pilots. "Use your harpoons and tow cables. Go for the legs. It might be our only chance of stopping them."

Luke ordered one of the Rebel speeders to set its harpoon. The speeder moved in on one of the walkers, and fired its harpoon and cable into one of the legs of the walker. Then the speeder began to circle around the feet of the walker, its cable trailing behind.

Once, twice, three times, the speeder wound its cable around the legs of the giant walking robot. Then the speeder detached the cable and zoomed away. Luke and the other pilots watched as the enormous legs of the walker attempted another step. No sooner had it done so than it began to lose its balance and teeter. It toppled and crashed into the icy ground. A second later it exploded .

"Good work!" Luke told the other pilots.

Luke teamed up with another snowspeeder and headed toward more of the giant walkers. Then, without warning, his speeder was hit with a laser blast.

"I've been hit!" he yelled into his comlink. He struggled with his controls, but it was no use. His ship went down, hitting the icy ground hard.

Smoke and fire exploded inside the cockpit of Luke's speeder. Dazed, Luke looked up just in time to see one of the giant walkers pounding toward him. He quickly unstrapped himself and pressed a button. The cockpit hatch sprung open. Luke leaped out of the snowspeeder seconds before the walker's giant feet crushed the speeder flat.

As the walker passed by, Luke fired a harpoon into its underside. Then he pulled himself up into the walker on a cable attached to the harpoon. He planted a bomb inside the walker and fled, leaving the bomb to destroy the giant robot.

Finally, Luke returned to the Rebel base where pilots were boarding their X-wing fighters and taking off into space. R2 had already prepared Luke's fighter.

"R2, get her ready for take-off," said Luke as he climbed inside his ship. Normally, he would have rejoined the other X-wing fighters. But the strange message from Ben Kenobi was still in his thoughts. He reset the ship's controls.

R2 responded with a series of worried bleeps. "There's nothing wrong, R2," said Luke. "Just setting a new course. We're going to the Dagobah system."

And with that he double-checked his readouts and took off.

Inside the Rebel base Han Solo and Princess Leia raced toward the *Millennium Falcon*. Imperial troops, led by Darth Vader, had penetrated the base and were capturing any Rebels they could find.

Han led Leia up the ramp and into the cockpit of the *Falcon*. C-3PO hurried behind. Inside, Chewbacca was already preparing for lift-off, but one of the controls was giving him trouble.

"This bucket of bolts is never going to get us past that blockade," said Princess Leia worriedly.

"This baby's got a few surprises left in her, sweetheart," replied Han as he strapped himself into the pilot seat and flipped some switches. The engine roared to life. "See?"

"Someday you're going to be wrong and I just hope I'm there to see it," taunted Leia.

Seconds later, just as some stormtroopers entered the docking bay, the *Falcon* lifted off and escaped through the main hangar door.

But no sooner had they reached orbit than they were confronted by two Imperial Star Destroyers.

"Check the deflector shields!" Han ordered Chewbacca. Chewbacca replied with a roar that the deflector shields were down. Han had no choice. He would have to try to outmaneuver the two immense battleships.

Han piloted the *Falcon* straight down between the two Star Destroyers. The Imperial ships veered toward the *Falcon*. Then Han instantly swerved off, leaving the two great crafts nearly to collide into one another.

"Prepare to make the jump to light-speed!" ordered Han.

Chewbacca entered the coordinates into the computer.

"They're getting closer!" Princess Leia exclaimed. Two more Star Destroyers were on their tail.

"Oh, yeah? Watch this!" replied Han, a gleam in his eye. And with that he flipped a switch on the controls and waited for the ship to jump into hyperspace.

Only nothing happened.

"Watch what?" asked Leia, rolling her eyes in disbelief. So far nothing Han had tried had worked.

Han groaned. "I think we're in trouble," he said. Even *he* was worried now. The Imperial ships were gaining fast.

Just then they felt the ship jolt. Something had hit them from outside. Looking through the viewport they saw a field of asteroids. There were hundreds of them, large and small.

Thinking quickly, Han reset the controls. But instead of flying away from the asteroid belt, he steered the *Falcon* straight toward it.

"What are you doing?" asked Leia, astonished. "You're not actually going into an asteroid field?"

"They'd be crazy to follow us, wouldn't they?" replied Han.

Han used all his skill as he piloted the *Falcon* around the oncoming asteroids. Behind them, three TIE fighters followed in hot pursuit. One of them scraped an asteroid and went hurtling out of control.

"We're going to get pulverized if we stay here much longer," warned Princess Leia.

"I'm going closer to one of those big ones," said Han.

"Closer?" Leia asked with surprise.

"Closer?" C-3PO repeated, terrified.

An asteroid about the size of a small moon loomed straight ahead. Han steered the *Falcon* toward it and began to skim along its surface. Before long, he spotted a giant crater and lowered the *Falcon* into it. Once they were inside the crater Han landed the ship and shut off all its power.

For the time being, Han hoped, they would be safely hidden from the Imperial fleet.

Darth Vader sat alone in a private chamber aboard his Star Destroyer and waited. He had received word that the Emperor was trying to reach him. After a few short moments, the Emperor, his cloak and hood barely hiding a horrible, ugly face, appeared to him. Vader sank to his knees.

"What is thy bidding, my Master?" Vader asked.

"There is a great disturbance in the Force," said the Emperor. "We have a new enemy — Luke Skywalker. The son of Skywalker must not become a Jedi. He could destroy us."

"If he could be turned, he would become a powerful ally," suggested Vader.

"Yes." The Emperor smiled. He liked the idea. "Can it be done?"

"He will join us or die, Master," promised Vader.

Far across the galaxy, Luke Skywalker had to force a landing on the cloud-covered planet of Dagobah. The atmosphere of Dagobah was so dense that Luke could not get clear readings on his X-wing's control panels. The landing was rough, leaving the starfighter half-submerged in a swamp. When Luke emerged from the ship he saw that Dagobah was a planet shrouded in dense fog. There seemed to be nothing but twisted trees and marsh for kilometers around.

"Now all I got to do is find this Yoda, if he even exists," Luke muttered as he and R2 made their way across the swampland. "It's really a strange place to find a Jedi Master. This place gives me the creeps. Still, there's something familiar about this place. I feel like — "

"Feel like what?" came a strange voice from within the fog.

Luke spun around, grabbing for his blaster as he turned.

Standing right in front of him was a strange, green-colored creature not more than a meter tall.

"Like we're being watched!" Luke said to the creature.

For a moment Luke felt silly as he brandished his laser pistol. Dressed in nothing but rags, the creature didn't look threatening at all.

"Away put your weapon!" demanded the small creature. "I mean you no harm."

Luke cautiously put away his blaster.

"I am wondering," asked the creature. "Why are you here?"

"I'm looking for someone," replied Luke. "I'm looking for a great warrior."

The small creature laughed and shook his head. "Wars not make one great," he said. Then, with the aid of his little walking stick, the creature began poking at a case of supplies that Luke had brought along. Something seemed to interest him: a tiny power lamp.

"Hey, give me that!" demanded Luke, reaching for the lamp.

"Mine!" insisted the creature, pulling the lamp close to his chest. "Or I will help you not."

"I don't want your help," said Luke. After several attempts Luke saw that it was useless to try to get his lamp back. He urged the little creature to go.

"Stay and help you, I will," insisted the creature as he eyed his new prize. "Find your friend."

"I'm not looking for a friend," explained Luke. "I'm looking for a Jedi Master."

"Ohhhh, Jedi Master," said the creature with a nod. "Yoda. You seek Yoda."

"You know him?" Luke asked.

"Take you to him, I will," said the creature. "But now we must eat."

And with that the little creature led Luke and R2 to his home: a strange mud hut that sat on the edge of a small lagoon. There, the creature prepared an exotic dinner.

"I just don't understand why we can't see Yoda now," griped Luke, impatiently. "How far away is Yoda? Will it take us long to get there?"

The little creature sighed and threw up his hands. "I cannot teach him," he said aloud. "The boy has no patience."

"He will learn patience," replied the voice of Ben Kenobi from out of nowhere. "Was I any different when you taught me?"

Luke spun around, confused. Ben was nowhere to be seen.

Suddenly it dawned on Luke that the little creature was none other than Yoda, the Jedi Master himself.

"He is not ready," Yoda said to Ben.

"Yoda, I am ready," insisted Luke. "I've learned so much."

Yoda sighed. "Will he finish what he begins?" he asked Ben.

"I won't fail you," Luke promised Yoda. "I'm not afraid."

Yoda slowly turned toward Luke. "Yeah, you will be," he warned the eager boy. "You will be."

And so the little creature agreed to begin Luke's Jedi training.

"There's something out there!" exclaimed Princess Leia as she rushed into the cabin of the *Millennium Falcon*. "Outside, in thc cave."

Han, Chewbacca, and C-3PO momentarily stopped their repair work on the *Falcon* and listened. Now they, too, could hear a sharp banging on the hull of the ship.

They went outside to investigate. A dark, leathery, two-meter-long creature had attached itself to the hull of the ship and was chewing on one of the power cables.

"Mynock," said Han, identifying the creature. He fired his laser pistol at it and it fell to the ground. But no sooner had Han fired his blaster than a whole swarm of ugly mynocks swooped through the air.

Suddenly the asteroid cavern began to shake and buckle.

All at once it seemed to grow smaller, as if it were closing in all around them.

"The cave is collapsing!" shouted Leia as she and the others retreated back into the *Falcon*.

"This is no cave!" exclaimed Han.

And that's when they saw that the opening of the cave was not made of jagged rocks, but of giant teeth. They were in the belly of a giant space slug. And its mouth was closing on the tiny ship.

Han rolled the *Millennium Falcon* on its side as it zoomed toward the monster's mouth. Then the *Falcon* made its way through the gigantic white teeth just before the huge jaw slammed shut.

But no sooner had they left the moon-sized asteroid than the *Falcon* was once again face to face with an Imperial Star Destroyer.

"Let's get out of here!" ordered Han. "Ready for light-speed?" Han pulled back on the hyperspeed throttle. Once again nothing happened.

Han thought quickly. "Turn her around," he commanded. He decided to face the Star Destroyer head on. The *Falcon* made a steep, twisting turn and raced straight toward the Star Destroyer. The *Falcon* bobbed and weaved, narrowly escaping several attacking laser blasts from the huge Imperial battleship. Han then found a small, empty spot on the hull of the Star Destroyer and landed the *Falcon*. They clung there like a bat, hidden from all sensors.

"What did you have in mind for your next move?" asked Princess Leia.

"They'll dump their garbage before they go to lightspeed," explained Han. "Then we just float away."

"With the rest of the garbage," agreed Leia. "Then what?"

"Then we find a safe port somewhere," answered Han as he began searching his star charts.

Just then Chewie barked that the Star Destroyer was beginning to move. Han detached the *Falcon* from the hull of the Imperial ship and they floated into deep space. Then he plotted a new course, headed for a planet he had located on his star charts. The planet was governed by his old friend, a gambler named Lando Calrissian. Han was certain he could make it to the planet safely. He just wasn't as certain he could trust Lando Calrissian.

Luke Skywalker raced through the marshy forest of Dagobah as if it were an obstacle course. He climbed, flipped, and jumped his way through the maze of trees and fog. He did all this as Yoda clung to his back and whispered quietly in his ear. The little Jedi Master was telling Luke how a Jedi's strength flows from the Force. And that a Jedi had to beware of the dark side.

Yoda brought Luke to a stop at the bog where Luke's X-wing fighter had landed. By now the ship was almost totally submerged. Here Yoda instructed Luke to stand upside down on his hands. Then he had Luke use the Force to levitate some large boulders.

Just then R2-D2 began to beep frantically. Luke looked up just in time to see his X-wing fighter sink completely into the bog.

"Oh, no," said Luke. "We'll never get it out now."

"So certain are you," said Yoda. "Always with you it can't be done."

"Master, moving stones around is one thing," said Luke. "This is totally different."

"No!" Yoda said angrily. "No different! Only different in your mind."

Luke agreed to try to raise the spaceship from the bog. But try as he might he didn't have the strength to do so.

"You want the impossible," Luke said, lowering his head in disappointment.

After a moment, Luke heard another sound coming from the bog. When he looked up, he saw that the tiny Yoda had not only levitated the huge X-wing fighter out of the bog, but was now directing it majestically toward the shore.

For the rest of his stay Luke practiced hard. He tried his best not to let anything distract him as he concentrated on lifting objects with nothing but his mind.

All of a sudden he became very distressed. An image of Han and Princess Leia flashed through his mind. They were in great danger! He raced to his X-wing fighter and ordered R2 to fire up the converters.

"You must not go," said Yoda, fearful that Darth Vader would win Luke over to the dark side of the Force.

"But Han and Leia will die if I don't," insisted Luke.

And with that he took off, promising himself that he would someday return to Dagobah and finish his training as a Jedi.

The *Millennium Falcon* landed on the cloud city of the planet Bespin. When Han and the others climbed out of the ship they were greeted by a dashing man in a long, stylish cape. Han recognized Lando Calrissian at once.

"How you doing, you old pirate?" Lando asked, cheerfully embracing Han. "What are you doing here?"

"Repairs," answered Han.

Lando led Han and the others across a narrow bridge and down the corridors of a brightly lit building.

C-3PO lagged behind, eyeing each nook and cranny of the building with curiosity.

All of a sudden C-3PO heard a familiar series of electronic beeps coming from inside a room. He went to investigate. Inside the room was a droid that reminded him of his companion, R2-D2. The unit wasn't alone, however. There was an Ugnaught junk worker inside the room as well. A feeling of dread filled C-3PO. Before he could escape, someone aimed a laser pistol at him and fired.

Outside, Lando led Han and Leia to a comfortable room that overlooked the beautiful cloud city. There the weary Rebels washed up and rested. After a while Leia became concerned about C-3PO. The droid had been gone too long to have gotten lost.

Just then Chewbacca entered the room. In his arms was a pile of golden junk that had once been C-3PO. Chewbacca explained that he found the droid in a junk room.

A short while later, Lando returned and invited them for refreshments. He led them to a huge doorway at the end of a corridor. But when the doors slid open Han and the others gasped with shock. Sitting at the end of a long banquet table was Darth Vader. And standing at his side was Boba Fett, a bounty hunter who intended to sell Han to Jabba the Hutt.

"We would be honored if you would join us," Vader said with a menacing laugh.

"I had no choice," Lando explained to Han, helplessly. "They arrived right before you did. I'm sorry."

Han threw Lando a mean look. "I'm sorry, too," he said, feeling betrayed. Then two Imperial soldiers took Han to a torture chamber.

A few hours later, when the soldiers were finished with Han, they threw him into a large cell along with C-3PO, Leia, and Chewbacca. By now Han was weak and pale from hours of interrogation. But no sooner had he rejoined his friends than Lando entered the room.

"Get out of here, Lando!" Han shouted angrily.

"Vader has agreed to turn Leia and Chewie over to me," said Lando, holding his ground. "They'll have to stay here, but at least they'll be safe." Then he said that Han was going to be turned over to the bounty hunter, Boba Fett.

"Vader wants us all dead," said Leia.

"He doesn't want you at all," explained Lando. "He's after somebody called Skywalker."

Han and Leia looked at each other. It was a trap, they realized. A trap for Luke.

More soldiers arrived as Han and Leia were led out of the cell and into a huge, noisy room of hissing pipes and steam. In the center of the room six Ugnaughts were frantically preparing a gigantic machine. The machine had a coffin-like container that looked as if it were designed to be lowered into a steaming pit.

Darth Vader and Boba Fett stood patiently by while the machine was being readied.

"What's going on . . . buddy?" Han asked Lando sarcastically.

"You're being put into carbon freeze," replied Lando. Leia gasped. Chewbacca roared in protest. C-3PO, who had been partially reassembled and was now strapped to Chewbacca's back, trembled with fear.

Han felt the grip of the Imperial guards tighten on his arms as they led him into the carbon freeze chamber. He fought back his fear and looked at Leia.

"I love you," she shouted to him, finally admitting her feelings.

"I know," Han said bravely. And with that he let himself be placed inside the coffin-like chamber and lowered into the steamy depths of the carbon freeze machine.

Minutes later the casket was lifted out of the freezing pit. Han, an expression of pain hardened across his face, was now a frozen slab of carbon.

"He's all yours, bounty hunter," Darth Vader told Boba Fett. The greedy bounty hunter happily carted Han away to his starship.

"Skywalker has just landed," an Imperial soldier announced to Vader.

"Good," replied Vader. And with that he ordered that Leia and Chewbacca be taken to his ship, breaking his promise to Lando. It was clear he was using them as bait to trap Luke.

Luke climbed out of his X-wing fighter and looked around at the beautiful cloud city. His landing had been easy, too easy, he thought, as he and R2 moved carefully down a deserted corridor.

No sooner had he turned a corner than he saw Leia, Chewbacca, C-3PO, and Lando Calrissian being herded along by several Imperial stormtroopers.

"Luke!" Leia shouted a warning. "It's a trap! A trap!"

Before she could finish, the stormtroopers whisked her and the others away through a doorway. Luke and R2 raced after them, but by the time they reached the end of the hall Leia and the others were nowhere to be seen.

Luke wandered off in search of his friends. He came upon an immense door and went through it. Behind was the carbon-freezing chamber. Luke was momentarily awed by the size of the giant black machinery.

Just then he saw something move above him on a walkway. It was a figure dressed in black. It was Darth Vader.

"The Force is with you, young Skywalker," said Vader. "But you are not a Jedi yet."

Luke ignited his lightsaber defiantly. A second later Vader responded by igniting his. Luke lunged, but Vader blocked the blow. Then Luke attacked again, successfully driving Vader back.

"Your destiny lies with me, Skywalker," Vader said to Luke as they fought.

"No!" exclaimed Luke.

But Vader attacked Luke mercilessly. Finally Luke felt himself being pushed into the steaming pit of the carbon freezer. He fell for several meters before closing his eyes and summoning the power of the Force. Before long he was able to reverse direction, shooting straight up out of the pit.

"Obi-Wan has taught you well," Vader told him, surprised. "You have controlled your fear. Now release your anger. Only your hatred can destroy me."

But Luke refused to give in to the dark side. He somersaulted over Vader and skillfully blocked the dark lord's sword blows. Vader lost his balance and fell through a maze of steam pipes and out of sight.

Leia, Chewbacca, C-3PO, and Lando followed as the Imperial soldiers led them to Darth Vader's ship. As they rounded a corner, a team of Lando's men jumped the stormtroopers and took away their weapons.

But before Lando could lead Leia and the others to the *Millennium Falcon*, Chewie grabbed him by the throat.

"Do you think that after what you did to Han we're going to trust you?" Leia asked Lando.

"I had no choice," Lando said, choking. "There's still a chance to save Han!"

Leia realized she would have to trust Lando this time if they stood any chance of rescuing Han. She ordered Chewbacca to release him. Then they raced to the landing port. But they were too late. Boba Fett had already loaded Han's carbon-frozen body onto his ship and was taking off when they got there.

Just then Imperial soldiers rushed in and began firing at Leia and the others. The Rebels had no choice. They would have to escape in the *Millennium Falcon* now and find a way to save Han and Luke later. They raced up the ramp of the *Falcon* and lifted off into the cloudy sky of Bespin.

Luke followed after Vader, walking cautiously along a tunnel until he came to a large reactor room. Reaching a window, he heard the sound of footsteps and turned. It was Vader.

Suddenly a pipe came hurtling at him from nowhere. Using the Force, Luke sent the pipe flying away from him. But Vader had command of the Force as well, and was using it to hurl object after object at the young warrior. Luke was no match for Vader's strength. One of the pipes went crashing through the window, carrying Luke along with it.

Outside the reactor room, Luke landed on a platform. Wind gusted all about him. Above him was nothing but endless space. Below was an enormous exhaust shaft, a bottomless pit.

Vader followed after, slashing at Luke with his lightsaber. One blow found its mark, slicing into Luke's right hand and knocking his lightsaber into the depths below.

"You are beaten," Vader said as he approached Luke. "There is no escape. Join me and I will complete your training."

"I will never join you!" vowed Luke.

"If you only knew the power of the dark side," said Vader. "Obi-Wan never told you what happened to your father."

"He told me you killed him." replied Luke.

"No," said Vader. "I am your father."

Luke was stunned. So stunned he nearly lost his footing.

"That's not true!" he shouted, crying. "That's impossible!"

"Luke, join me and together we can rule the galaxy as father and son," said Vader.

"No! No!" cried Luke. And with that he jumped off the platform and let himself be sucked deep down the shaft.

Luke tumbled and tumbled until finally he emerged at the undermost part of the cloud city. If he had not reached out and grabbed a thin electronic weather vane, he would have plummeted to his death on the gaseous planet below.

Luke tried to pull himself up on the weather vane, but the great gusting winds of Bespin's atmosphere kept pushing him down. Closing his eyes he called for help.

He began to think of Leia. He had had a vision of her once when she was in trouble. Perhaps he could send a similar vision to her, wherever she was.

"Leia," he cried out, concentrating. "Leia . . ."

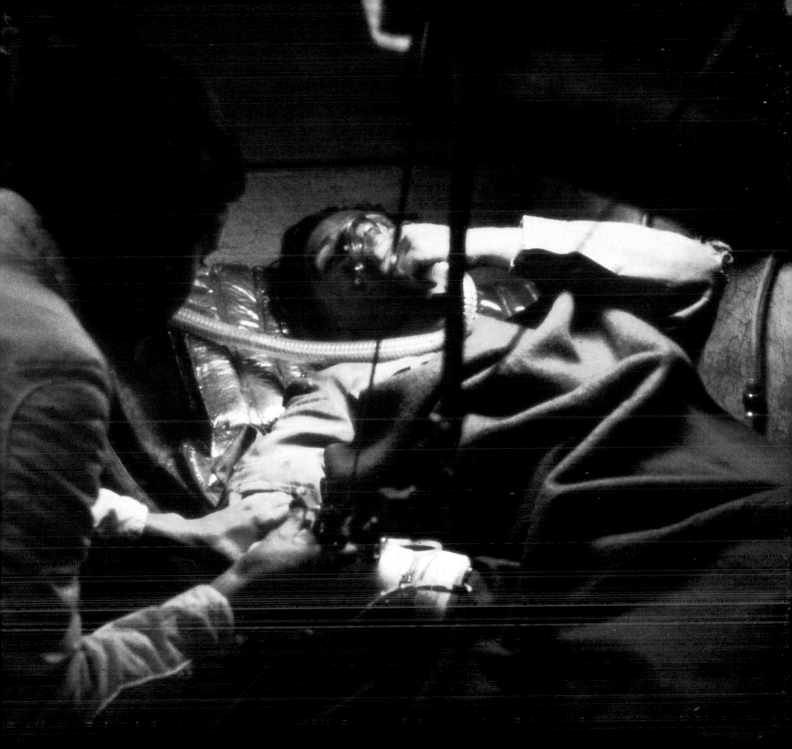

He focused with all his power, his body shifting in the wind as he did so. Soon he felt himself growing weaker. He wouldn't be able to hold on much longer, he knew. His head reeled.

Suddenly Luke felt himself being scooped up as if by a giant hand. It was the *Millennium Falcon*, its top hatch wide open to receive him. Inside were Lando Calrissian, Chewbacca, and Princess Leia. She had heard his cries after all!

Minutes later R2-D2 had repaired the *Falcon*'s hyperdrive. The *Millennium Falcon* jumped to lightspeed and raced away from Bespin.

As *the* **Millennium Falcon** *jumped through the dimensions of hyperspace,* **Luke Skywalker** *sighed with relief. For the time being he and the others were safe. But what of Han? Was he all right, he wondered. Would they ever be able to rescue him?*

And what of Darth Vader, thought Luke. Was the evil lord of the Empire truly his own father? And if that were so, would Luke be able to destroy him in order to save the galaxy?

Luke stared out into the empty vastness of space and hoped the answers to these questions would come to him soon. For he knew that the fate of the universe hung in the balance . . .

TO BE CONTINUED . . .